The Arapaho

Hunters of the Great Plains

by Karen Bush Gibson

Consultant:
Frances Merle Haas
Sky People Higher Education
Ethete, Wyoming

Capstone press
Mankato, Minnesota

Capstone Press,
151 Good Counsel Drive, P.O. Box 669, Mankato, Minnesota 56002.
www.capstonepress.com

Library of Congress Cataloging-in-Publication Data
Gibson, Karen Bush.
    The Arapaho: Hunters of the Great Plains/by Karen Bush Gibson.
    p. cm. — (American Indian nations)
    Summary: Provides an overview of the past and present lives of the
Arapaho people, tracing their customs, family life, history, culture, and
relations with the United States government.
    Includes bibliographical references and index.
    ISBN-13: 978-0-7368-1564-2 (hardcover)
    ISBN-10: 0-7368-1564-3 (hardcover)
    ISBN-13: 978-0-7368-4821-3 (softcover pbk.)
    ISBN-10: 0-7368-4821-5 (softcover pbk.)
    1. Arapaho Indians—Juvenile literature. [1. Arapaho Indians.
2. Indians of North America—Great Plains.] I. Title. II. Series.
E99.A7 G53 2003
978'.004973—dc21   2002011999

Editorial Credits
Charles Pederson, editor; Kia Adams, designer; Alta Schaffer, photo
researcher; Karen Risch, product planning editor

Photo Credits
Capstone Press/Gary Sundermeyer, 13
Corbis, 28, 33, 38
The Denver Public Library, 19
Marilyn "Angel" Wynn, cover (main and inset), 4, 9, 10, 14, 16, 20, 24–25, 30,
    34, 40, 42, 44, 45
National Cowboy and Western Heritage Museum, Oklahoma City, OK, 37
North Wind Picture Archives, 22–23, 26

1 2 3 4 5 6 08 07 06 05 04 03

Table of Contents

Features

Like Harvey Spoonhunter, pictured above, more than 7,000 people consider themselves to be Arapaho. Many Arapaho people celebrate their heritage by dancing at powwows.

Chapter One

Who Are the Arapaho?

The Arapaho are an American Indian nation. They have made their homes in the Great Plains area of the central United States for at least 300 years. During this time, the Arapaho moved often. This nomadic tribe followed herds of buffalo from Canada to Colorado and back again.

Today, many Arapaho live in Wyoming and Oklahoma. The Wind River Reservation in Wyoming is home to the Northern Arapaho. Many Southern Arapaho live in western Oklahoma. The 2000 U.S. Census shows 7,000 people consider themselves Arapaho.

No one knows for sure how the nation came to be known as Arapaho. They call themselves hiinono'eino', which means "roaming people." Scholars believe the name "Arapaho" comes from the Pawnee Indian word "tirpihi," which means trader. Other tribes of the Great Plains knew the Arapaho as good traders.

Another possible source of "Arapaho" is the Crow word "alappahó." This word means "people with many tattoos." Long ago, Arapaho men and women wore circular tattoos. They used cactus points to prick the skin and then rubbed powdered charcoal into the wounds.

The Arapaho have long lived in an area of weather extremes, the Great Plains. These flatlands extend from the Mississippi River to the edge of the Rocky Mountains. These mountains and hills provided shelter from strong winds on the plains. Temperatures may be very hot or very cold. During the winter, the temperature may be as cold as minus 30 degrees Fahrenheit (minus 34 degrees Celsius). During the summer, the temperature may be higher than 100 degrees Fahrenheit (38 degrees Celsius). Rainfall may be light or heavy. Drought is a serious problem in some years.

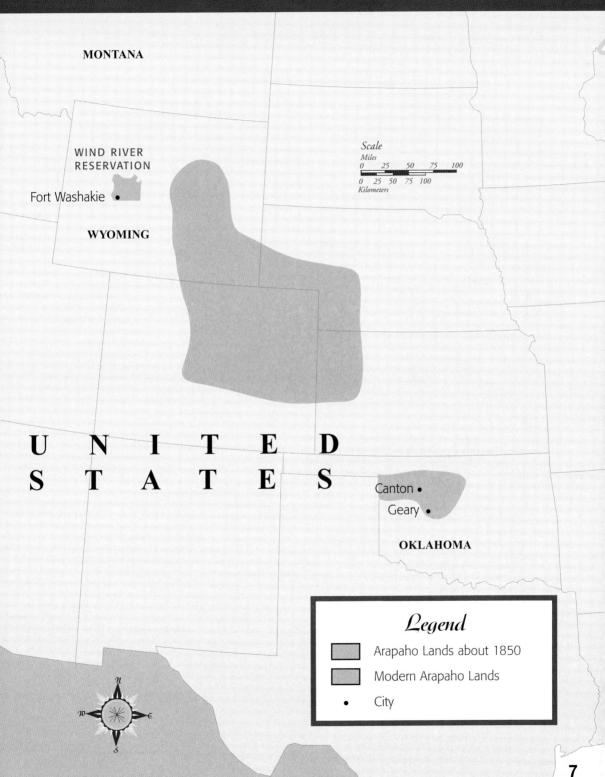

MONTANA

WIND RIVER
RESERVATION

Fort Washakie

WYOMING

Scale
Miles
0   25   50   75   100
0   25   50   75   100
Kilometers

U N I T E D
S T A T E S

Canton
Geary

OKLAHOMA

Legend

Arapaho Lands about 1850

Modern Arapaho Lands

• City

N
W   E
S

The Arapaho language belongs to the Algonquian group of languages. Speakers of Algonquian languages first lived in the northeast United States. The Algonquian tribes of the Arapaho, Cheyenne, and Blackfeet migrated from the forested lands in what became the eastern United States and Canada. Hundreds of years ago, these tribes moved west onto the Great Plains, where they still live. Today, Arapaho people speak English, but some also speak their native language.

Northern Arapaho may work for the tribal government or a gas station, grocery store, bingo hall, or one of the other tribal businesses. When work is hard to find on the reservation, Arapaho sometimes look for jobs in neighboring towns and cities. Southern Arapaho may work as farmers or ranchers or may look for work in nearby Oklahoma City. Unemployment is high among the Arapaho.

The Arapaho have preserved their traditions and customs. They attend ceremonies or powwows to share stories, food, dancing, and singing. They practice traditional ceremonies and beliefs. The Arapaho are proud of their past and look forward to the future.

The Wind River Reservation in Wyoming features rivers and steep hills. The reservation is part of traditional Arapaho land.

Arapaho on the Great Plains lived in homes called tepees. Tepees were made from buffalo skins stretched over tree poles. The tepee below was made in the late 1800s.

Chapter Two

Traditional Life

No one knows when or why the Arapaho moved to the Great Plains. One clue about their past is their Algonquian language. It proves the Arapaho once lived between the East Coast of the United States and the Great Lakes area. Other Algonquian speakers lived in this same area.

Early Arapaho may have lived in dome-shaped homes called wigwams. The wigwams may have been in farming villages where the Arapaho grew corn and other crops. American Indian historians explain that some Arapaho moved in search of better food sources. Other Arapaho moved away from enemy tribes. Their easily movable homes on the plains were called tepees.

The Arapaho were one of the earliest tribes to migrate to the Great Plains. By the 1700s, they had settled near the Missouri River and had begun to trade with nearby farming tribes. One of these tribes was the Hidatsa. They called the Arapaho "bison-path people" because the Arapaho followed the bison, also called buffalo.

The Importance of Horses

Spanish explorers brought horses to the Americas in the 1500s. They traded the horses to southwestern Indian tribes.

In the 1730s, the Arapaho probably traded buffalo meat and buffalo skins for their first horses. The Arapaho also may have stolen horses from neighboring tribes like the Shoshone.

Horses made hunting easier. Before they had horses, the Arapaho had to sneak up on buffalo to shoot them with arrows. Horses let hunters ride alongside the buffalo to shoot them.

Horses also made moving easier. Before the Arapaho had horses, they used dogs to help move their belongings from place to place. The Arapaho used a sled made for dry land. This travois was attached to a dog. The dogs then pulled tepees and other belongings. A strong dog could pull about 75 pounds (34 kilograms). Later, the Arapaho used horses to pull their travois. Horses could pull several hundred pounds.

Buffalo Jerky

The Arapaho depended on the buffalo for food, shelter, and tools. Because the Arapaho moved often, they needed healthy food that could be stored easily. Hunters easily could take buffalo jerky on hunting trips. You can make this recipe with buffalo meat or beef jerky. Ask an adult to help you when slicing meat and using the oven.

Ingredients
1 pound (455 grams) buffalo meat or
  very lean beef
1 tablespoon (15 mL) salt
½ teaspoon (2.5 mL) black pepper

Equipment
sharp knife for slicing
large sealable plastic freezer bag
baking sheet
aluminum foil

meat rack
pot holders
fork

What You Do
1. Partially freeze meat up to an hour to make slicing easier. Preheat oven to 175°F (80°C). Cut meat diagonally across the grain for pieces that are 6 inches (15 centimeters) long, 3 inches (7.5 centimeters) wide, and ⅛ to ¼ inch (.3 centimeters to .6 centimeters) thick. Cut away fat.
2. Place meat slices, salt, and pepper into plastic bag. Seal tightly and shake. Remove meat from bag.
3. Line baking sheet with aluminum foil. Place a meat rack on top of the pan. Spread out the slices of meat on the rack.
4. Cook 2 hours. Turn meat over and cook another 2 to 3 hours, until it is dry and chewy.

Serves 6 to 8

The Importance of Buffalo

The buffalo provided the Arapaho with many things they needed for daily life. They used nearly every part of the buffalo. They ate the meat, made tools from many body parts, and made clothes from the hair and skin.

Buffalo hunting was important to the Arapaho. A popular hunting method was to frighten buffalo into running over a

Arapaho painted the buffalo hide above. It shows Arapaho using horses during a buffalo hunt.

cliff. Another way to hunt was to chase the buffalo into a narrow canyon with a pen at the end. Either way, the hunters could kill as many buffalo as they needed. The Arapaho hunted on foot until they learned to ride horses.

To follow the herds of buffalo, the Arapaho lived in easily movable tepees. Tepees were made of about 15 to 20 buffalo skins draped over several poles. An opening in the top of the tepee allowed smoke from cooking fires to escape. The tepee door faced east to catch the rays of the rising sun.

Traveling over the Great Plains, the Arapaho met many other tribes who also depended on buffalo. Arapaho often met their friends the Cheyenne and Sioux and their enemies the Shoshone and Ute. Enemies often fought over horses or hunting territories.

The buffalo and other animals provided clothing as well as food and shelter. During the coldest months, buffalo skins provided warmth. Men wore deerskin leggings and shirts. They also wore a waist covering made of cloth or animal skin called a breechcloth. Women wore dresses and leggings of animal skins. Soft leather from deerskin was used to make moccasins with tough rawhide soles. The Arapaho decorated their clothing with painted designs. Before Europeans arrived,

The Arapaho made leather clothing from animal skins. The dress above has beadwork decorations.

the Arapaho dyed porcupine quills to decorate their clothes. Later, they traded with Europeans and Americans for beads. The Arapaho sewed these beads into patterns on their clothes.

Family Life

Large groups of Arapaho traveled in spring or summer. Since feeding smaller groups was easier, the tribe split into smaller bands during the winter months, when food was scarce.

The Arapaho hunted and gathered much of their food. Men hunted buffalo, deer, elk, and other animals. Women gathered wild fruits and vegetables.

Games taught children about life. Boys ran, used bows and arrows, and played war games. These activities taught skills the Arapaho valued in hunters and warriors. The games taught the boys to work as a team.

A teacher taught older boys songs and dances as they learned hunting and fighting skills. Groups of boys trained together and promised to help each other throughout their lives.

Girls also learned skills as children. They often played with dolls to learn how to care for children. At the age of 12, girls lived with a grandmother or other adult female. They learned to skin buffalo and cook food for their families.

Marriage

Arapaho marriage was not complicated. When an Arapaho man wanted to marry, he and his family brought horses for the woman and her family. To accept the marriage, the woman's family also presented the man's family with gifts.

The families set up a tepee for the couple. Both families feasted in the new home. Older Arapaho leaders prayed and offered advice for a successful marriage. After the feast, the families exchanged more gifts. The Arapaho then considered the couple married.

The Stages of Life

The Arapaho believed they traveled through four stages, or hills, of life. These stages went along with the four directions of east, south, west, and north. They also went with the four seasons of spring, summer, autumn, and winter. The four stages of life were childhood, youth, adulthood, and old age.

Each stage of life had certain duties. People had to pass a series of tests at one stage before they could enter the next stage. The Arapaho respected older people because they had lived longest and had the most experience. After traveling the four stages, the Arapaho believed they could be reborn.

Adulthood was the third stage of Arapaho life. As warriors, adult men protected the people.

Arapaho and their Cheyenne allies visited Bent's Fort to trade with soldiers and settlers.

Chapter Three

The United States Brings Change

In the mid-1700s, the Arapaho met English traders along the Saskatchewan River in Canada. By the late 1700s, Arapaho often came in contact with trappers near the Rocky Mountains. The Arapaho began to trade with settlers like William and Charles Bent. These two brothers built a trading post called Bent's Fort in present-day Colorado.

In 1803, the U.S. government bought the Louisiana Territory from France. This area included most of the Great Plains. Explorers Meriwether Lewis and

William Clark set out to explore farther west. More white settlers and explorers soon followed. Trappers looked for beaver skins. Miners wanted gold. Settlers looked for land. These growing numbers of people disturbed the lives of the Arapaho.

Early in the 1800s, the Arapaho split into two groups. The Northern Arapaho enjoyed the cooler mountain climate. They lived near the source of the Platte River in present-day Wyoming. The Southern Arapaho preferred the warmer weather near the Arkansas River in Colorado. Although the Northern and Southern Arapaho lived on different parts of the plains, they continued to gather for ceremonies and visits with relatives.

Indian-White Relations Become Worse

The United States won the Mexican War (1846–1848) and claimed land in the American Southwest. People began traveling to California to look for gold, which was discovered there in 1848.

Around this time, increasing numbers of American settlers traveled the Oregon-California Trail through Wyoming.

In 1850, the Arapaho and other Indians of the plains met with U.S. government members at Horse Creek, Colorado. The government asked that settlers be allowed to cross "Indian Country." In return, no white settlements or towns

During the 1840s and 1850s, settlers entered Indian land. Indian nations sometimes attacked them. The Arapaho usually had peaceful relations with settlers.

could be built on the Great Plains. Both sides signed the Horse Creek Treaty. The treaty placed borders on the land the different tribes would control. The Arapaho shared land with the Cheyenne east of the Rockies. Their land lay between the North Platte and Arkansas Rivers.

Many settlers and traders ignored the Horse Creek Treaty. This was especially true when gold was discovered at Pikes Peak, south of Denver, Colorado. The Arapaho protested, but the United States did nothing to back up Arapaho rights stated in the treaty.

Mining settlements and towns began to develop on Arapaho land. Denver and other towns made gathering more difficult for the Northern and Southern Arapaho. The Indians had to pass through areas where miners lived. These Americans did not like having so many Indians nearby. The Northern and Southern groups became separate from each other.

The Sand Creek Massacre

In 1860, large numbers of settlers moved onto Arapaho land. They outnumbered the Arapaho 10 to one. They wanted Arapaho land. In Colorado, the local militia and volunteers

Colorado militia troops attacked Arapaho under government protection. The attack was called the Sand Creek Massacre.

attacked peaceful Cheyenne and Arapaho villages. Some warriors from these nations in turn attacked settlers.

Other Arapaho asked the U.S. Army for protection in what was becoming a dangerous situation. They did not want to fight. They gave their weapons to the army. These Arapaho camped with the Cheyenne at Sand Creek near Fort Lyon, Colorado. Both a white flag of peace and a U.S. flag flew over

White hunters sometimes traveled by train to find buffalo herds. They shot large numbers of buffalo. As the number of buffalo decreased, the Arapaho had trouble surviving.

the chief's tepee. These flags showed that the people in the camp were supposed to be under government protection.

On November 29, 1864, the Colorado military under the command of Colonel John Chivington attacked the camp. The soldiers ignored the U.S. flag, the white flag, and a flag of surrender the Arapaho and Cheyenne raised as the fighting began. The soldiers killed 200 Arapaho and Cheyenne. Many men were away from the camp hunting, so most of the victims were women, children, and older people. This Sand Creek Massacre upset not only American Indians, but also people throughout the United States.

Little Food

During the 1860s, Northern Arapaho warriors joined the Northern Cheyenne and Sioux against Americans. In 1862, the discovery of gold in Montana brought more U.S. settlements and military forts. From 1865 to 1868, the Arapaho and other groups fought settlers and the U.S. Army. Many people on both sides died. Indians who lived through the attacks found their homes burned. Most of their food was burned or taken. They struggled to find enough food.

The loss of the buffalo was even more difficult than battles with settlers and the army. Before white people arrived, buffalo

Chief Little Raven

Chief Little Raven led the Southern Arapaho during a difficult time in Arapaho history. He was born in the 1820s and spent much of his life keeping peace between his tribe and white settlers. Little Raven earned a reputation as a warrior in battles against the Sauk and Fox Indian nations. In 1855, he became a chief.

Little Raven lived through the Sand Creek Massacre. He did not trust the fort commanders and had camped away from the main Arapaho group. When the fighting occurred, he helped some of his people to safety.

Little Raven was persuasive. In 1867, he attended the Medicine Lodge Creek Council. He convinced the government to give the Southern Arapaho land in Oklahoma. The president wanted to give Little Raven a medal for making peace, but Little Raven said he had never been at war with white people. In 1871, he spoke about peace between the Arapaho and the United States to crowds in Boston, New York, and Washington, D.C.

Chief Little Raven spent the last years of his life helping his people adjust to reservation life in Oklahoma. In 1889, he died in Oklahoma.

herds were so big they looked like dark blankets moving across the plains. Plains tribes hunted what they needed. They used every part of the buffalo. But white hunters killed large numbers of buffalo. They often took only the hides and left the meat to spoil. In 1804, about 60 million buffalo roamed the plains. By the 1860s, the buffalo were almost gone.

Between the battles and the loss of the buffalo, the Arapaho found life difficult. Many of them starved. Others died from smallpox and other diseases introduced by white settlers. The U.S. government urged various Plains Indian nations to live on lands set aside for them. These lands were called reservations.

Reservation Life

In 1867, the Southern Arapaho attended the Medicine Lodge Creek Council. They asked for reservation land. By 1869, Chief Little Raven of the Southern Arapaho had persuaded U.S. President Ulysses S. Grant to give the Arapaho land in western Oklahoma. The Southern Arapaho settled with the Southern Cheyenne near the North Canadian River. They tried to adapt to a life of farming.

In the late 1860s, the Northern Arapaho settled on the Sioux Reservation in Wyoming. In 1874, the U.S. Army and a band of Shoshone attacked the Northern Arapaho. Many

Arapaho died in battle. Many who lived starved or froze during the following winter.

The surviving Northern Arapaho were able to adapt. Their leaders convinced the U.S. Army to hire Arapaho as scouts. The scouts received military pay and supplies that they shared with the members of their nation.

Getting food was a continual challenge for the Arapaho. Government Indian agents sometimes stole food meant for the

Many Arapaho children attended Carlisle Indian School in Pennsylvania. The students pictured above are studying in the school's library.

Arapaho. They sometimes gave the Arapaho rotten food. The agents resold the good food and kept the money themselves.

Poor reservation conditions further lowered the number of Arapaho. In eight years, the Northern Arapaho population dropped from 972 people to 823.

In 1878, the Northern Arapaho agreed to move onto the Wind River Reservation in Wyoming. They shared the land with the Shoshone.

Becoming like White People

The U.S. government wanted the Plains Indians to become more like white people. The government passed laws that said the Arapaho could not hold ceremonies or meet in groups. No more than four families could camp or live together. Families were not allowed to visit each other.

To receive an education, Arapaho children had to attend live-in boarding schools. Children were forced to leave their families to study at these schools. Some children went as far away as Carlisle Indian School in Pennsylvania. Indian students had to dress, speak, and act like white Americans. They could not speak their native language or perform traditional acts.

Broken Promises

In 1887, the U.S. government passed the General Allotment Act. This law broke earlier treaties about land different tribes controlled. The law split reservations into smaller lots for families. The government sold the leftover land to settlers. The Southern Arapaho were forced to sign agreements giving each family only 160 acres (65 hectares). By April 1892, about 30,000 settlers had entered Cheyenne and Arapaho land.

As the 1900s began, Southern Arapaho faced poverty and the loss of their lands. White Americans stole Arapaho land and animals. By 1920, settlers claimed half the Arapaho land. By 1928, the Southern Arapaho had only 37 percent of their original land.

In 1934, the U.S. Congress passed a law called the Indian Reorganization Act. The law returned land to Indians. It also promised that allotments would not occur again.

The Arapaho tried to regain their original reservation land. The Southern Arapaho were unable to win back their original land. By 1947, the Northern Arapaho of the Wind River Reservation gained control of money from the sale of some of their land. They bought back as much land as they could. Today, they own more than 2 million acres (809,400 hectares). They used the rest of the money to build homes and bring electricity to the reservation.

Edward Curtis took the picture of the Arapaho man pictured above in 1910. Curtis traveled the West, taking photos at about the time whites were taking Arapaho land.

Many modern Arapaho, like the jingle dancer shown here, gather to dance and hold ceremonies.

Chapter Four

The Arapaho Today

Today, many Arapaho people live in Oklahoma and Wyoming. In Oklahoma, Southern Arapaho live in either tribal housing or private homes in Geary, Canton, and other small Oklahoma towns.

The Wind River Reservation in Wyoming is home to about 6,500 Northern Arapaho. The Northern Arapaho tribal headquarters is located on the reservation at Fort Washakie.

Both Northern and Southern Arapaho have had trouble finding good jobs. Some Arapaho are considered poor. Few tribal or reservation jobs exist. Many Arapaho have moved to nearby towns to find work.

Northern Arapaho

Education is important to the Arapaho. Northern Arapaho attend tribal public schools. There, students learn about Arapaho customs and language. More than 60 percent of Northern Arapaho complete high school. About 6 percent complete college. In school year 2001–2002, the Northern Arapaho Sky People Higher Education Program provided scholarships to 200 college students. In 1998, the Higher Education Program of the Cheyenne-Arapaho of Oklahoma provided scholarships for 205 college students.

The Northern Arapaho share their reservation with the Shoshone. But the two governments are separate from each other. All Arapaho 18 years of age and older belong to the General Council. This group makes all large decisions and elects a six-member business council every two years.

The Arapaho Business Council works with the Shoshone council to manage the Wind River Reservation. The business council also manages Arapaho programs and businesses. One of the first Arapaho tribal businesses, a cattle ranch, began in 1940. Other tribal businesses today include a gas station, grocery stores, a bingo hall, and a truck stop. Many new businesses begin every year.

Carl Sweezy

Carl Sweezy was born in 1879 on the Cheyenne-Arapaho reservation near Darlington, Oklahoma Territory. Sweezy also was known as Wattan, meaning Black. He was one of the first American Indian artists to use a style of painting that tells a story.

As a boy, Sweezy enjoyed drawing. He later learned to paint with watercolors. He attended the Carlisle Indian School.

At age 20, Sweezy worked for James Mooney, a scientist at the Smithsonian Institution, located in Washington, D.C. Mooney studied the Cheyenne-Arapaho. He needed an artist to rework paint on old shields and to copy other designs of Arapaho art. Sweezy did the work.

In 1920, Sweezy began painting as a full-time career. His paintings have provided details and information to modern scholars about Arapaho dress, rituals, and ceremonies. In 1930, Sweezy painted *Peyote Road Man*, shown here. It can be found in the National Cowboy and Western Heritage Museum in Oklahoma City, Oklahoma.

On May 28, 1953, Sweezy died in Lawton, Oklahoma. Today, the National Museum of the American Indian, other museums, and individual collectors own Sweezy's work.

Northern Arapaho elders on the Wind River Reservation designed a flag to honor Arapaho soldiers who had died for the United States during World War II (1939–1945). The flag was introduced in 1956 but never officially adopted. Some Arapaho use the flag today.

The flag contains seven stripes of white, red, and black. White stands for a long life. Red is for the Arapaho people.

In 1900, Southern Arapaho and Cheyenne council members met together in Oklahoma.

Black means happiness. A white triangle with black edges contains a red and black circle separated by a white line.

Southern Arapaho

During the late 1800s and early 1900s, the Southern Arapaho lived with the Southern Cheyenne. These groups lived under laws that allowed white people to take their land.

Today, only 15 percent of that original land remains with the Southern Arapaho. Oil and gas companies pay to use some of that land. Farmers and ranchers also rent land. The money earned from renting supports tribal programs and government. Tribal businesses also help support the tribe.

In 1936, the Cheyenne and Arapaho began a business council, located in Concho, Oklahoma. Tribal members elect four Arapaho and four Cheyenne to the council. The council governs the Southern Arapaho and Cheyenne.

Today, census counts group the Southern Arapaho and Cheyenne together. The Oklahoma Office of Indian Affairs lists 11,418 Cheyenne-Arapaho people.

The Cheyenne and Arapaho of Oklahoma designed a blue flag with a spear and two sets of 14 feathers. The feathers represent the old tribal council of 14 members. The flag shows the seal of the two groups in front of a map of Oklahoma. An arrow pointing down represents peace. A peace pipe symbolizes religious beliefs.

The sketch artist above and other Arapaho artists pass on Arapaho traditions through their artwork.

Chapter Five

Preserving the Traditions

The Arapaho people have worked hard to preserve the traditions and customs of their people. Artists pass on tribal knowledge by creating images of traditional life. The people teach their children the Arapaho language and customs in reservation schools. Arapaho on the Wind River Reservation also practice traditional religion in addition to Christianity.

One of the most difficult tasks has been preserving the Arapaho language. Many Arapaho children did not learn their language. They attended boarding schools where they could not speak it. In the

1940s, a man named Zdenak Salzmann came to Wyoming to study the Arapaho language. After many years, Salzmann and others developed a written Arapaho language. In 1979, people finally agreed on spelling rules. Having written and spoken forms of Arapaho has made the language easier to teach and learn.

Both the Northern and Southern Arapaho hold powwows during the summer months. A powwow is a gathering of

Arapaho boys enjoy playing a game of basketball. The Arapaho value their children, who are the future of their people.

Shinny

Like many other American Indian tribes, the Arapaho played a stickball game much like present-day field hockey. The Arapaho called their stickball game shinny. Two teams played against each other on an area of ice in winter or flat ground in other seasons. The teams used a curved stick to hit a ball to each other and to pass it across a goal line. There was no limit to the number of people who could play shinny. The game had no rules except that players could use only the stick to touch the ball. Today, women sometimes sew shinny balls from deerskin, and children still play shinny at Arapaho gatherings.

people for dancing, drumming, and singing. In September, the Arapaho hold a powwow with their Cheyenne neighbors. During powwows, Arapaho children may play a stickball game called shinny. They also enjoy other games during the powwows.

Families are important to the Arapaho. The people respect the elders of the nation. Through storytelling, these older leaders teach values, beliefs, and tribal history. Children then can know and understand their history. They can pass it on to their children and grandchildren.

Arapaho Timeline

The Sand Creek Massacre occurs.

The Northern Arapaho settle on the Wind River Reservation with the Shoshone people.

1803   **1864**   **1869**   **1878**

The United States buys the Louisiana Territory from France; the purchase includes Arapaho land.

The Southern Arapaho move to Oklahoma with the Southern Cheyenne.

The U.S. Congress passes the General Allotment Act.

The Northern Arapaho introduce but do not adopt an official flag.

| 1887 | 1930s | 1956 | 1979 |

The Arapaho adopt a written language.

The Indian Reorganization Act ends allotment and puts tribal land in trust. The Northern Arapaho regain most of their land.

Glossary

allotment (uh-LOT-muhnt)—an official distribution

breechcloth (BREECH-kloth)—a waist covering made of cloth or animal skin

ceremony (SER-uh-moh-nee)—a traditional ritual that marks or celebrates an important occasion

moccasin (MOK-uh-suhn)—a soft leather shoe

tepee (TEE-pee)—a cone-shaped tent made of animal skins

travois (truh-VOY)—a vehicle of two joined poles carrying something and pulled by a horse or dog

Internet Sites

Track down many sites about the Arapaho. Visit the FACT HOUND at *http://www.facthound.com*. IT IS EASY! IT IS FUN!

1) Go to *http://www.facthound.com*
2) Type in: 0736815643
3) Click on "FETCH IT!" and FACT HOUND will find several links hand-picked by our editors.

Relax and let our pal FACT HOUND do the research for you!

Places to Write and Visit

Cheyenne and Arapaho Tribes
Tribal Headquarters
P.O. Box 38
Concho, OK 73022

Northern Arapaho Tribe
P.O. Box 396
Fort Washakie, WY 82514

The Southern Plains Indian Museum
P.O. Box 749
U.S. Highway 62 East of Anadarko
Anadarko, OK 73005

For Further Reading

Sita, Lisa. *Indians of the Great Plains.* Traditions, History, Legends, and Life. Milwaukee: Gareth Stevens, 2000.

Stefoff, Rebecca. *The Indian Wars.* North American Historical Atlases. Tarrytown, N.Y.: Benchmark Books, 2002.

Terry, Michael Bad Hand. *Daily Life in a Plains Indian Village, 1861.* New York: Clarion Books, 1999.

Index